S0-BSA-614

TRAPPED
in Space

by David Johnson
Illustrated by Sonny Liew

Librarian Reviewer
Marci Peschke
Librarian, Dallas Independent School District
MA Education Reading Specialist, Stephen F. Austin State University
Learning Resources Endorsement, Texas Women's University

Reading Consultant
Elizabeth Stedem
Educator/Consultant, Colorado Springs, CO
MA in Elementary Education, University of Denver, CO

 STONE ARCH BOOKS
Minneapolis   San Diego

First published in the United States in 2007
by Stone Arch Books, A Capstone Imprint
151 Good Counsel Drive, P.O. Box 669,
Mankato, Minnesota 56002
www.capstonepub.com

First published by Evans Brothers Ltd,
2A Portman Mansions, Chiltern Street,
London W1U 6NR, United Kingdom

Copyright © 2003 Evans Brothers Ltd

Library of Congress Cataloging-in-Publication Data
Johnson, David, 1948 Mar. 1–
  [Space Explorers]
  Trapped in Space / by David Johnson; illustrated by Sonny Liew.
  p. cm. — (Shade Books)
  First published: London: Evans Brothers Ltd., 2003 under the title
Space Explorers.
  Summary: Stranded when their shuttlecraft crash lands while
they are helping to explore a new planet, teen siblings Sammi and Jak
are saved from deadly plants by intelligent beings who communicate
primarily through shared feelings.
  ISBN-13: 978-1-59889-354-0 (library binding)
  ISBN-10: 1-59889-354-8 (library binding)
  ISBN-13: 978-1-59889-449-3 (paperback)
  ISBN-10: 1-59889-449-8 (paperback)
  1. Brothers and sisters—Fiction. 2. Extraterrestrial beings—Fiction.
3. Poisonous plants—Fiction. 4. Outer space—Exploration—Fiction. 5.
Science fiction. I. Liew, Sonny, 1974– ill. II. Title.
PZ7.J631631149Tra 2007
[Fic]—dc22   2006026878

Art Director: Heather Kindseth
Graphic Designer: Kay Fraser

Printed in the United States of America in Stevens Point, Wisconsin.
            012011   006049R

Table of Contents

CHAPTER 1

The Spears

The aircraft rose into the air, then zoomed across the wide plain, leaving the camp behind it. The ground below was covered with brown grass. Prickly trees grew in clumps. A wide river looped across the plain.

Sammi and her brother, Jak, lived on a huge spaceship called the *Titan*. Their mother and father were scientists. The ship explored new planets, looking for worlds for people to live on.

Younger children weren't allowed on the surface of unknown planets. But Sammi and Jak were teenagers, and were allowed to come down in the shuttle to help the scientists with their work.

"Thanks for taking us on the trip, Chad," said Sammi. Chad was a pilot. He had been sent off in a jet-powered helicopter called a buzzer. His job was to find some plant samples. He had asked Jak and Sammi to come along.

"Hope you like the ride," said Chad. "We won't be gone long, because I like to fly this baby really fast."

The base camp was near the river. The first team to arrive had set up buildings for the scientists to work in, and a landing field for the shuttle.

This planet had some strange life on it, including deadly spear plants. The plants had already killed one scientist. They looked harmless, but when someone came near them, the plants fired sharp spears at the person. Then the plants sent out long suckers to feed on the dead body.

Chad pointed out a place where spear plants grew. The plants had fat brown trunks about three feet tall, and thick leaves. Some of them had red flowers. Sammi knew they were just plants, but she still felt as if the evil little trees could think.

"I'll fly a little lower, but not too low," Chad said. "I don't want to take any chances."

"Hey, look at that!" cried Jak. The plants under the buzzer had fired off their spears.

They shot up, curved over the buzzer, and fell toward the ground. Luckily the aircraft was out of range.

"The noise of the buzzer must have triggered them," said Chad.

The buzzer reached the edge of the plain, where a steep cliff rose up. A waterfall tumbled down the cliff. Soon the buzzer was crossing a land of hills.

The hills were rough and rocky, but there were many deep valleys, green with plant life. Huge red birds soared over the jagged rocks.

"Hey!" Jak shouted. "What's that over there?"

A gray creature was lying in the sunshine. It was hard to see it because it blended in with the planet's gray rocks.

Chad flew lower. The creature looked like a shaggy dog with three horns on its head. When it heard the buzzer, it stood up on two legs and ran down into the valley. It was about six feet tall.

Suddenly there was a bang. The aircraft lurched sideways. Chad pulled hard on the controls. The engine sounded like it was coughing. The aircraft just barely cleared the rocks at the top of the valley. The next valley was wider.

Chad spotted a flat piece of ground. "Hang on, we're going down!" he shouted.

He landed the buzzer as carefully as he could, but one side of the flat ground was soft and swampy. The aircraft tipped over. The engine stopped with a final sputter.

Chad jumped out of the buzzer and looked underneath it.

"What happened?" Sammi called.

A long green pole was sticking into the base of the machine.

"We must have passed over a spear plant in that valley. This spear's gone right through the engine. I am so stupid!" Chad said angrily.

Sammi climbed out. "How will we get back?" she asked.

"We won't, not in this machine. I'll have to radio back to the camp." Chad groaned. "I'm going to be in so much trouble over this! I'll get yelled at by the captain in the morning!"

Jak climbed out of the buzzer. "Are there any spear plants around here?" he asked.

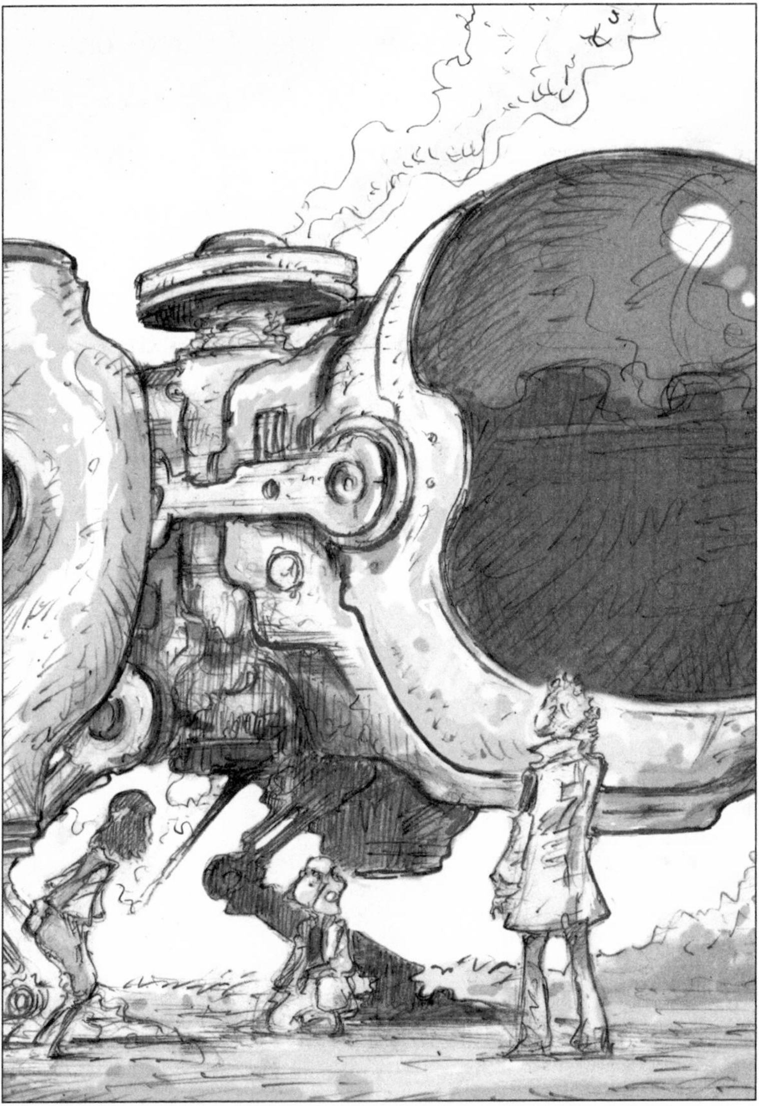

"Yes," Chad said. He pointed. "There's one over there. It fired at us when we came down. Don't worry, though. Once they've fired their spears, it takes them a few days to grow new ones."

Chad climbed back into the buzzer and picked up the radio. "Buzzer nine to base camp. Chad Mason here. We have problems. Come in, please."

Nothing but a hiss came from the machine. Chad tried again. "Come in, base," he said louder.

Again, there was no reply. Sammi had a horrible feeling. Would they have to walk back? What about the spear plants out on the plain?

"Is the radio broken?" she asked.

"No. It's this deep valley. The radio signals are being blocked. Now, I want you to wait here and keep the doors shut. I'm going to take the radio to the top of the hill," Chad said. He jumped out of the buzzer and started to climb the hill.

Two hours went by. Sammi and Jak waited.

Chad still hadn't come back, and the day was coming to its end.

CHAPTER 2

Night Strangers

Night was falling, and Jak and Sammi were still alone.

"What are we going to do now?" said Jak.

Sammi didn't know. She couldn't imagine what had happened to Chad.

"Chad must be in trouble. We have to go and look for him," Jak told her.

Sammi agreed. "We'll climb up the hill to see what happened."

Sammi opened the door and stepped out into the squelchy mud. Jak jumped down beside her. Nearby was the spear plant. Sammi was glad it had used up its spears. Its big flower buds waved gently even though there was no wind.

One of the buds was almost open. Yellow pollen drifted from it.

The children smelled a strange perfume. Suddenly everything seemed to become hazy.

The yellow pollen reached Sammi first. She fell to the ground. Soon Jak was stretched out on the muddy grass next to her.

Sammi and Jak couldn't move. They felt sick and dizzy, but they were still awake.

Hours passed in the dark valley. Jak tried to pretend it was just a horrible nightmare.

Sammi thought about the spear plant.
Would they still be lying there when the plant
grew new spears?

She thought that she fell asleep for a while, and then woke up again. She was very cold. The sky was lighter now. The light came from the planet's two moons.

Then she heard a very quiet noise. It was as if something was creeping slowly toward her across the wet ground, making quiet sucking sounds.

Sammi remembered learning that the long roots of the spear plants survived by feeding on dead bodies.

What if this was a sucking root, creeping toward her across the mud?

Maybe, when the plants had fired all their spears, they used the strange pollen instead to catch their prey. But their victims were not dead, just paralyzed, waiting for the roots to get nearer and nearer.

For a moment the creeping sound stopped. Sammi tried to convince herself that it couldn't be a root. Nothing could grow that quickly, could it? But then it started creeping and sucking again, closer and closer.

Sammi couldn't scream out loud, but somehow she screamed in her head. Then she must have blacked out. The next thing she felt was her body being lifted up. She felt herself being put on a stretcher of some sort. She tried to speak, but her lips and tongue would not move.

She was carried for a long time. Then she felt the stretcher carefully being put down. She again fell into a deep sleep.

When she woke up, there seemed to be more light. Above her, Sammi could see a roof made of gray rock.

To one side there was a bright patch of light. It was the mouth of a cave. But what was she doing in a cave?

She looked again at the bright area of light, and as she did, a figure stepped into it.

It was tall, taller than anyone she had ever seen. And on its head were three horns.

CHAPTER 3

The Horned People

The creature was coming closer, blocking out more light.

Sammi sat up. Jak was fast asleep next to her. "Jak! Wake up! It's one of those horned things!" she whispered loudly.

Jak scrambled to his feet and started walking toward the horned being. He did not seem to be frightened.

This was too much for Sammi. It felt like a bad dream. Sammi screamed.

The creature knelt down on the floor, looking like an animal in pain. Could Sammi's scream have hurt it? It had shown signs of pain just before she had screamed. The creature turned and ran out of the cave.

"Why did you do that?" said Jak. "She was only trying to help us."

"How do you know? How do you know it's a she, anyway?"

"I just know," Jak said, shrugging.

"You can't know. They could kill us, eat us, or anything!" Sammi said.

"They won't. Come on, let's go and tell her it's all right," Jak replied.

Outside the cave, they saw that they were in a shallow valley.

Below them was a village. Small stone houses were scattered around a central square. The buildings were simple, but they were solid and well made, with wooden shutters on their windows.

A large, two-story building stood next to the square. A wide stream ran through the village. Many of the horned people were filling big pots with water from the stream. A group of children were splashing in it.

Jak thought of them as people rather than creatures. Sammi wasn't sure. Fear flooded her mind again. As if they could feel her fear, the whole village stopped what they were doing and turned to look at Jak and Sammi.

"Come on," Jak said, walking toward the village.

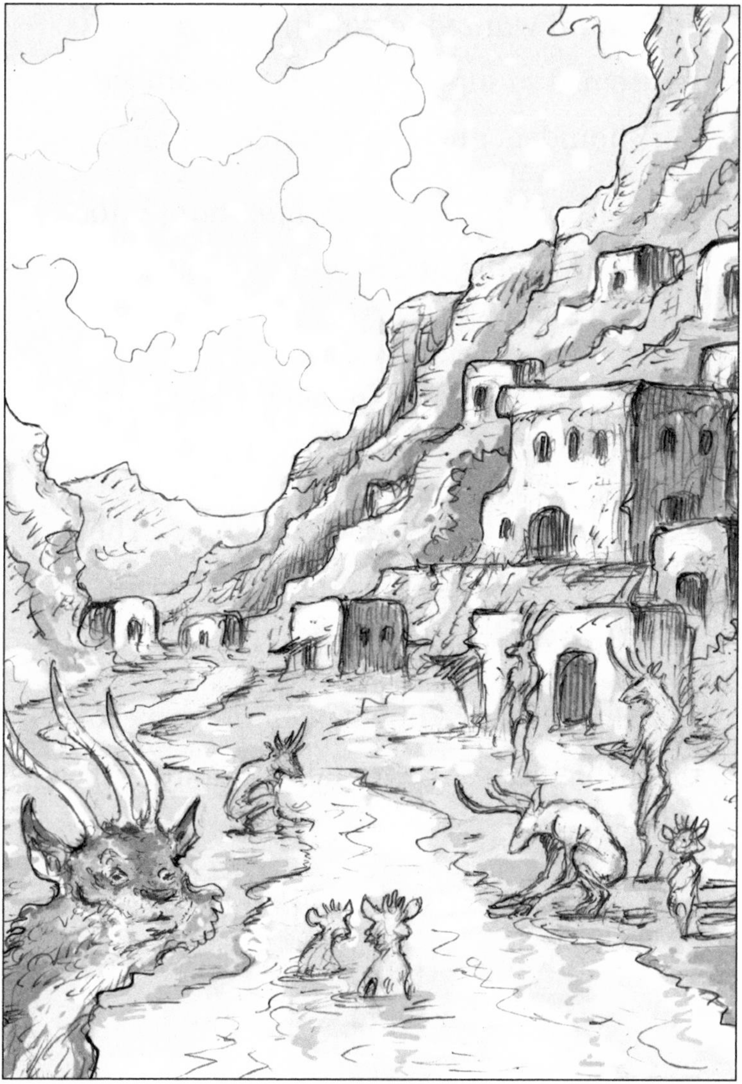

Sammi wanted to call him back, but he seemed so sure of himself. She shrugged her shoulders and followed him.

The horned people seemed happy to see them. Some of the young ones came running up.

Jak and Sammi were led to the square in the center of the village.

There were seats made of planks. They sat down and were surrounded by horned people of all ages.

"How do you know which ones are male and which ones are female?" Sammi asked Jak quietly.

"I just do," he said. He pointed to some of the children. "Those two are both boys, but that one over there is a girl."

Sammi was too polite to stare at the horned creatures, but there really didn't seem to be any difference. She wondered again how Jak was so sure.

In the middle of the square was a large fire. Two adults were putting a skinned animal onto a long pole. The animal was going to be cooked for supper.

Sammi felt sick. You didn't get fresh meat on space ships. It upset her to see an animal being roasted.

Sammi really wanted to find out how Jak seemed to know so much about these people. But he found it hard to explain.

"I just feel it in my head," he said.

"You mean you can read their minds?" Sammi asked, confused.

"No, of course I can't!" Jak said. It was difficult for Jak to explain what was happening to him. For some reason there was something that he could do, but that she could not.

"I just know they are friendly," he said. "And some of them are female and some male. I can't explain it. And they can feel what we are feeling. Like when you were upset in the cave. You were frightened and your feelings really hurt her."

Sammi still didn't understand. "Do you mean they can read our minds? That's horrible."

"No, I don't mean that," said Jak. "I don't think they can, anyway. They just feel things."

Jak wouldn't say any more.

Sammi was still not sure about the horned people. She also didn't like the idea of Jak being able to do something she couldn't. It made her feel left out.

* * *

It was after dark by the time the food was ready. Someone started cutting up the meat with a knife made from a sharp stone.

The two humans were each given a plateful of meat and vegetables. They were surprised by how good it was.

Sammi looked up. A bright dot was crossing the sky. It was the *Titan* in orbit. She felt even more lonely.

She began to cry quietly. Instantly the alien people all knew she was unhappy. They started to pat her face and arms.

Then something happened, the worst thing she could imagine. A loud roar echoed over the hills, and two new stars, red and flickering, rose into the sky.

"Those are the shuttles!" Sammi cried. "Oh no! They're going back to the *Titan*! How can they leave us behind?"

CHAPTER 4

The Storehouse

The horned people felt Sammi's terror. They all looked upset. Sammi and Jak were taken back to their cave, where their feelings of fear were blocked out by the thick rock.

Jak was angry. "Why did you do that? You upset them!"

"But the shuttles. Didn't you see? They took off without us!" Sammi said, pointing toward the sky.

"Dad would never let them do that," Jak said, confused.

Sammi agreed, but there had been no rescue party, no buzzers flying in the sky.

Sammi thought she wouldn't be able to sleep that night, but worrying made her tired. Soon she and Jak were asleep. Outside, the horned people had settled down again. One of them was playing a sad tune on a stringed instrument.

Suddenly, the sky was lit up by a flickering red light. It hung in the air, then died away. The whole village jumped up, pointing and speaking in their quiet voices. They had no idea what this strange light could be. Sammi and Jak would have known that it was a distress flare, but they were sleeping.

The next morning, Sammi and Jak came out of their cave. They expected the villagers to be angry with them, or even march them back to the cave. Instead everyone was friendly as Sammi and Jak made their way down the path.

They were hungry, and the horned people seemed to know. There was some greasy cold meat left over from the night before, and Sammi and Jak were given plates of it, along with what looked like lumpy soup. Even Sammi ate everything the horned people gave her.

They went for a walk around the village.

Jak seemed happy, but Sammi couldn't understand why. Didn't he realize that they could be trapped here on the planet forever?

"Jak, we can't just stay here. We've got to do something," said Sammi.

"Like what?" Jak asked.

"We could try to speak to them. Maybe they could help us look for Chad."

"But, Sammi, we don't know their language," Jak said.

"I know that," Sammi said. "But you seem to know what they're thinking. That's a start."

"I keep telling you, I don't know what they're thinking. Sometimes I can just tell what they feel," said Jak.

The female who had come to them in the cave when they had first woken up was especially friendly. From the way the other people acted, it seemed that the female was an important person.

Even Sammi could recognize her, because she had a red streak of fur on one arm.

As the two children walked back to the square, they met her. Sammi wanted to try speaking to her.

Sammi pointed to one of the houses and said, "House." Red Arm understood her right away. She pointed to the house and mumbled something. Sammi tried to say it back to her. But Red Arm didn't try to say "house."

Sammi tried again. She pointed to the cooking fire, and said, "Fire." She got a different mumble in return. This seemed to be an easier word, and Red Arm looked pleased when Sammi tried it. Sammi then pointed to her chest, and said, "Sammi." Red Arm pointed to her chest and made another whispering, mumbling noise. Sammi tried it.

Red Arm was interested now, although she didn't try to repeat any of Sammi's words. She pointed to her head, her arm, her horns, and her legs. Each time she made a different noise. Finally she tapped her chest and made the first sound again.

Sammi groaned. "That's not her name. It must be the word for chest she's saying. I'm not getting anywhere!"

Red Arm thought that the game was over. She patted Sammi on the arm, then disappeared into one of the houses.

Horned people came to their doors as Sammi and Jak walked past. Everyone was busy. Outside one house, clay pots were drying in the sun on wooden racks. Inside another, a loom could be heard as someone made blankets.

Sammi and Jak headed for the tall building by the square. The doors were open. People were sitting outside in the sunshine, some on benches, some on the ground. They were busy preparing food, mending blankets, and making tools out of wood and stone.

Sammi wondered whether they would be allowed inside the building. She peeked in. No one seemed to mind, so they went in.

The building was the village storeroom. The ground floor was stacked high with objects: a pile of spears, hides from animals, and stacks of tall jars containing seeds.

There were small windows all around, but it was gloomy. They almost didn't notice the familiar object lying in the middle of the floor.

It was the radio Chad had taken with him when he'd left them three days ago.

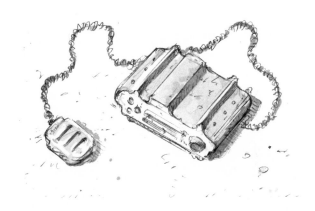

CHAPTER 5

Chad's Radio

"Chad's radio!" Jak shouted. "How did that get here?"

"I wish we knew how to work it," said Sammi.

"No problem," said Jak. "I've seen them used dozens of times."

They took the radio outside. Jak pressed one of the buttons.

"Anyone there? Come in, please," he said There was no reply.

"We might be on the wrong frequency," he said. There was a panel of buttons, but despite his boast, Jak had no idea what any of them did. He pressed one marked "out-station call."

A few moments later they heard a voice.

"Hello, who's there? This is Chad Mason, and I'm lost. Come in, please!"

"Chad, this is Jak! I'm here with Sammi. Where are you? Over."

"Jak! Are you two okay? You must have found the radio. I slipped on some rocks and banged my head after I left you. I dropped the radio and couldn't find it. I blacked out after that. When I woke up I was on a mountainside and there was no sign of the radio," Chad went on. "I've been lost for two days. Where are you?"

Sammi took over and tried to tell Chad their story. Of course they couldn't tell him where they were. They had no idea.

"How can you talk to us, Chad, if we've got the radio?" Sammi asked.

"I've got a pocket unit," Chad replied. "You must have pressed the call button, and it beeped at me. These units don't have a big range, so you can't be far away. Look for a switch called homing. Flip it on. My unit has got a direction finder so I can find my way to you."

Sammi found the button and pressed it. A few moments later Chad spoke again.

"I'm on my way!" he said.

Sammi said, "Chad, did you see the shuttles taking off last night?"

There was a pause. "Yes, I saw them. I'm not sure what's going on. Don't worry, I'll be with you as soon as I can."

Jak and Sammi decided to put the radio back in the storehouse. If they took it with them to the cave, the homing signal might be blocked.

Sammi spent the rest of the afternoon trying to talk to the horned people, but without much luck.

Jak had been thinking. "I think I know why you couldn't get Red Arm to say her name."

"Why?" Sammi asked.

"None of them have names," said Jak. "They don't need them, because they know each other by the way they think and feel."

"Why can't I tell what they're feeling?" Sammi asked.

"I don't know. I can only do it a little bit. I'm not very good at it. Maybe you need horns to do it really well," said Jak.

Evening came and the big fire was lit when the children heard a sound on the rocky path. The villagers jumped up in alarm and stood with their horns pointing in the direction of the sound.

Chad walked into the firelight, and then the alarm was over. The musician kept playing.

The villagers knew that Chad meant no harm, and that he was tired and hungry and thirsty.

Chad waved to Sammi and Jak. "Hi, guys! Is there any dinner left for me?"

One of the horned people brought a plate of food. Chad thanked them very politely, and although the villagers didn't understand Chad's words, his message was clear enough.

Chad was interested in how the horned people knew what they were feeling.

"We've come across people like this on other planets," Sammi said. "They're called empaths. They can't read minds, but they can tell when someone is hungry, or frightened, or in pain. They can find each other when they are in trouble. Jak can do it a little, even if he doesn't have horns."

Chad laughed. "Too bad! A couple of horns would look good on him."

"Why do you think the empaths didn't rescue you?" Sammi asked.

"They probably found you when I was knocked out," Chad said. "My brain wasn't sending out messages, I guess. The ones that found you must have found the radio. Anyway, where is it?"

They went to the storehouse and Chad checked the radio.

"Everything's working okay," he said. "I should be able to get a signal to the *Titan*, but I'll have to wait until it's overhead."

Chad set the radio up on a rock. He looked at his watch. "We should see the *Titan* in about five minutes," he said.

They waited five minutes, then ten, then twenty, but no bright light passed over the valley.

The *Titan* was no longer in orbit around the planet.

CHAPTER 6

On the March

The fire was dying down. The musician played a last, sad tune.

Sammi had a coldness in her stomach. She didn't want to upset the village people, so she went back to the cave, where her sadness would be blocked by the rocky walls.

After a while Chad and Jak joined her. Chad tried to be cheerful, but it was difficult when he couldn't understand why they had been left on the planet.

Suddenly there was a repeat of last night's flare, burning red in the dark sky.

Chad jumped up excitedly. "Hey, guys, it's a flare. Someone still loves us out there!"

Sammi and Jak ran to the cave's entrance, watching the flare dying away. They cheered and clapped their hands.

Most of the villagers had gone back to their houses. The villagers still sitting around the fire danced and waved too. Even the musician took out his instrument again and played a cheerful tune.

Chad checked the direction with his compass. "Now we know what direction to head in the morning. Get some sleep, you two. You're going to need it."

The next morning they were ready to leave the village of the horned people. A path climbed out of the valley going in the right direction toward their base camp.

The villagers seemed worried. They kept getting in the way. Soon Chad, Jak, and Sammi were surrounded by the horned people and couldn't move.

"What's going on?" said Chad.

The horned people wouldn't move. They simply stood there, mumbling quietly.

After a while, Chad and the children turned and walked back into the valley. The horned people moved away.

"They don't want us to go," said Jak. "They're protecting us. It's dangerous outside the valley. They don't want us to get hurt."

"Well, we can't stay here forever," said Chad. "We have to get back to camp. Just stroll around, then when I say go, rush for the path."

When Chad said, "Go!" they ran as fast as they could, but the villagers were quicker. A group of gray furry bodies was soon blocking the way.

Sammi became upset.

"Why won't you let us go?" she yelled, beating at one of the villagers with her fists. "Don't you understand? I want to go home!"

The horned people began to move away, some of them holding their horns. The three humans moved forward.

This time, no one tried to stop them.

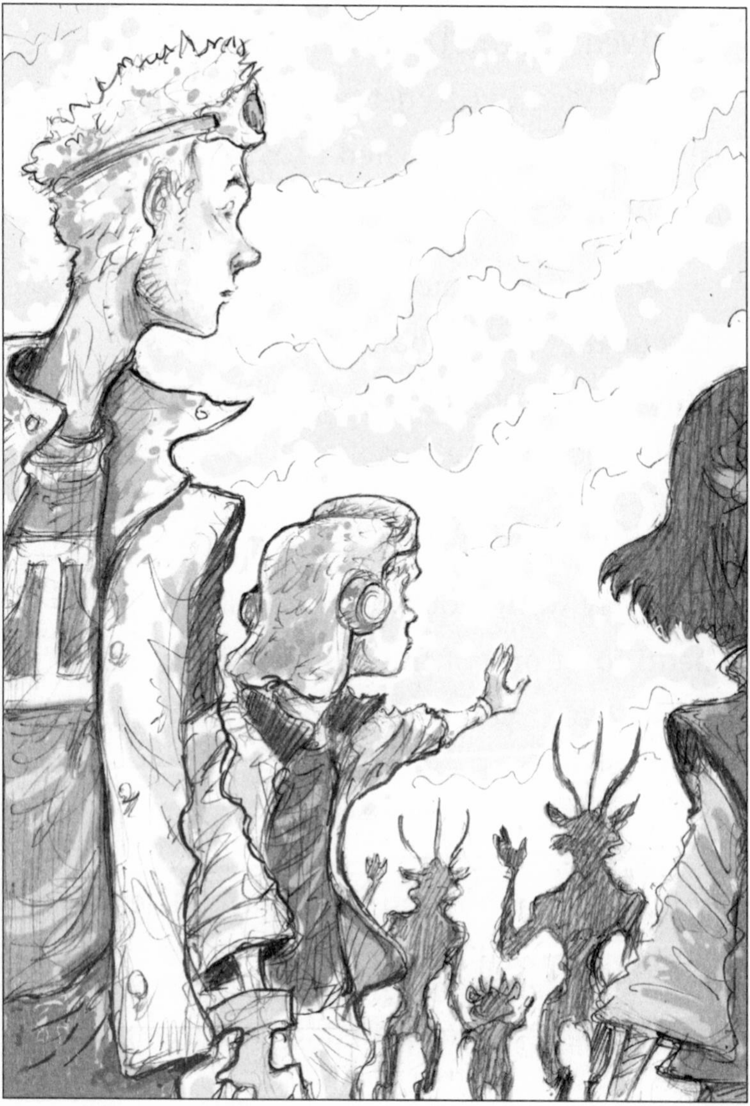

When they had climbed halfway up the hill, Jak stopped and turned. He raised his hand and waved. The horned people held up their arms, somehow knowing that it was the human way of saying good-bye.

Jak, Sammi, and Chad walked across a wide plain that was broken up by deep valleys full of spear plants. The plants were dangerous, so the humans tried to walk around them.

Although it was sunny, a cold wind was blowing. There were no paths to follow, but Chad kept them on track with his compass.

After walking for over three hours, they stopped for a rest. They had reached a pile of rocks that sheltered them from the wind. Chad handed out a bottle of water and some food pills.

"No sleeping," said Chad firmly. "I don't know how much farther we have to go and I don't like the idea of too many more nights out in this cold. Come on, let's move."

Jak put his hand down to push himself up. Suddenly he cried out in pain. "Something bit me!"

Chad grabbed Jak's hand, looking worried. Bites on unexplored planets could be serious. An angry red mark showed up on Jak's thumb. A scratching sound came from between the rocks and a small creature disappeared into the shadows.

Chad pulled a first-aid kit from his pack and wrapped a bandage on the thumb. "How does it feel?" he asked.

"It stings a little," Jak said.

They started walking again. After half an hour Chad stopped and checked Jak. He didn't like what he saw. Jak's hand was puffy, and red marks were spreading up his arm.

"How do you feel now?" Chad asked, trying to keep the worry from his voice.

"Okay, I think," Jak said softly.

After another ten minutes it was clear that Jak was in trouble. His arm was throbbing, and he felt dizzy.

"I need to sit down for a minute," he said.

"Okay," Chad said. "Take a break, you two. I'm just going over to that pile of rocks up ahead."

Jak lay down with his back against a smooth rock. He just wanted to curl up somewhere out of the cold wind and sleep.

Chad climbed up on the pile of rocks to get a view of what lay ahead. When he reached the top, he almost cheered. They had reached the edge of the hills. He could see the ground falling away to the wide plain with the broad river sweeping across it. In the distance was the site of the scientist's camp.

Something tall stood in the middle of the camp. It was one of the *Titan's* shuttles! But the camp itself looked empty. Where were the people?

With his binoculars, Chad looked at the path they would have to take. Across the wide plain, hundreds of spear plants stood like an army of deadly soldiers.

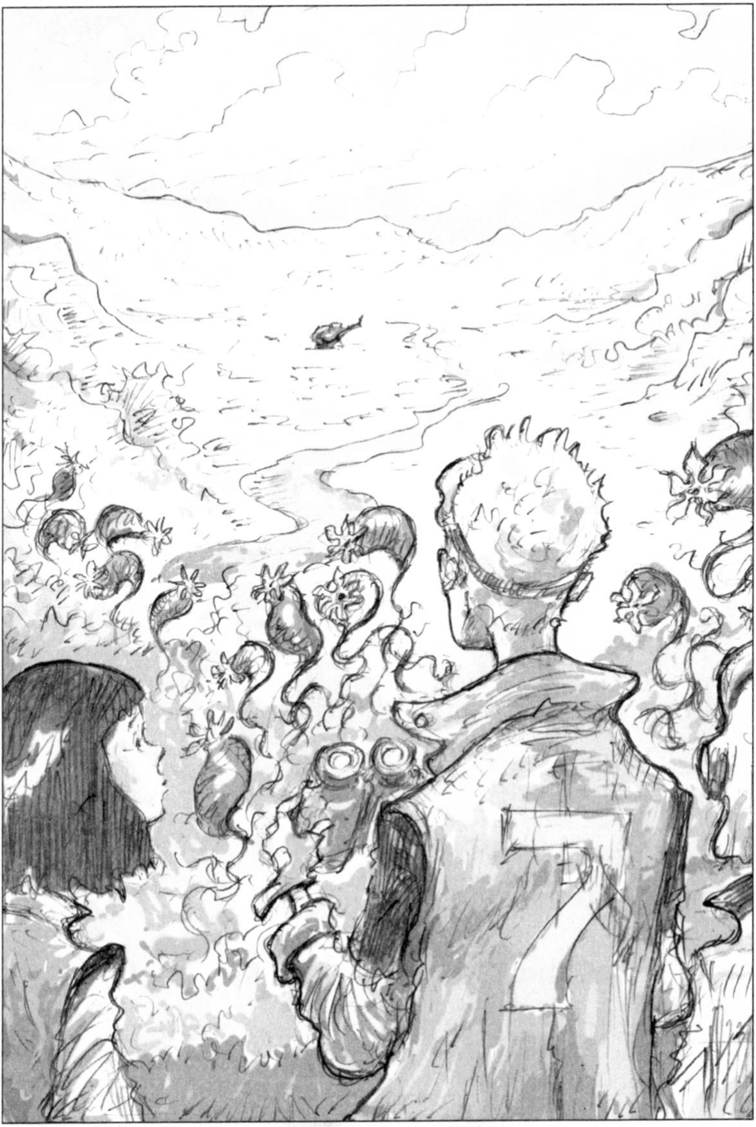

CHAPTER 7

Down the River

Chad guessed that the pollen from the spear plants had affected the camp, just as it had affected Sammi and Jak. He remembered how the flowers of the plants had been opening as they flew over them. It must have been the beginning of the flowering season.

The wind must have blown the pollen right into the camp.

When there was nothing but silence from the radio, Chad realized why no rescue party had been sent for them.

People left the camp to escape the pollen. The shuttle must have been left behind just in case Chad and the children were able to reach it. The nightly flare was automatic, set up to guide them back to camp.

Jak was sleeping now, shivering slightly.

"He's really sick, isn't he?" asked Sammi.

Chad nodded. "Yes, he's sick. But we're almost to the plain, and there's a shuttle for us at the base. But there's a problem."

He handed Sammi the binoculars. He wanted her out of the way for a while so that he could have a good look at Jak's arm.

Jak's whole arm was swollen. The red marks ran in streaks up to his elbow.

Jak opened his eyes.

"Does it hurt, Jak?" Chad asked gently.

Jak didn't speak. He just nodded, then closed his eyes again.

Chad heard footsteps. He thought Sammi had returned, but it wasn't Sammi.

It was Red Arm. Behind her stood two more horned people. The horned people had followed them all the way from the village. In all his years exploring strange planets, Chad had never met such caring people. If only humans could be more like them!

Red Arm kneeled down and looked at the red marks on Jak's arm. She looked at Chad, then moved the palm of her furry hand sharply across Jak's shoulder. Her meaning was clear. If Jak were to be saved, his arm would have to be cut off.

Then Sammi returned. For once she was pleased to see the horned people, especially Red Arm. Sammi trusted her.

"What was she trying to tell you?" she asked Chad.

"She thinks the arm will have to come off to save Jak," Chad said. He sighed. "Sammi, she's probably right."

"But how?" said Sammi. "There's no hospital here, and nothing for the pain. If only we could get Jak back to the *Titan*!"

Sammi started walking. She headed up the hill, waving at Red Arm to make her follow. When they got to the top, Sammi pointed toward the distant shuttle, and with all her heart she longed to be back at home on the ship. Red Arm gazed across the plain, and slowly she understood.

Red Arm led them down the cliff. A stretcher had been made for Jak from a blanket and two spears. The two other horned people carried him between them.

When they reached the bottom of the cliff, Red Arm turned sharply to the right, following a new path. They heard water splashing ahead.

The group squeezed between two boulders and saw a waterfall tumbling down the cliff and into a large pond. In the pond were three boats. They looked like canoes.

Chad and Sammi got into one of the boats. Jak was gently laid into another. One of the horned people traveled with Chad and Sammi, Red Arm was in Jak's boat, and the third horned person traveled alone in the last boat. Each boat had a paddle that was covered with animal fur.

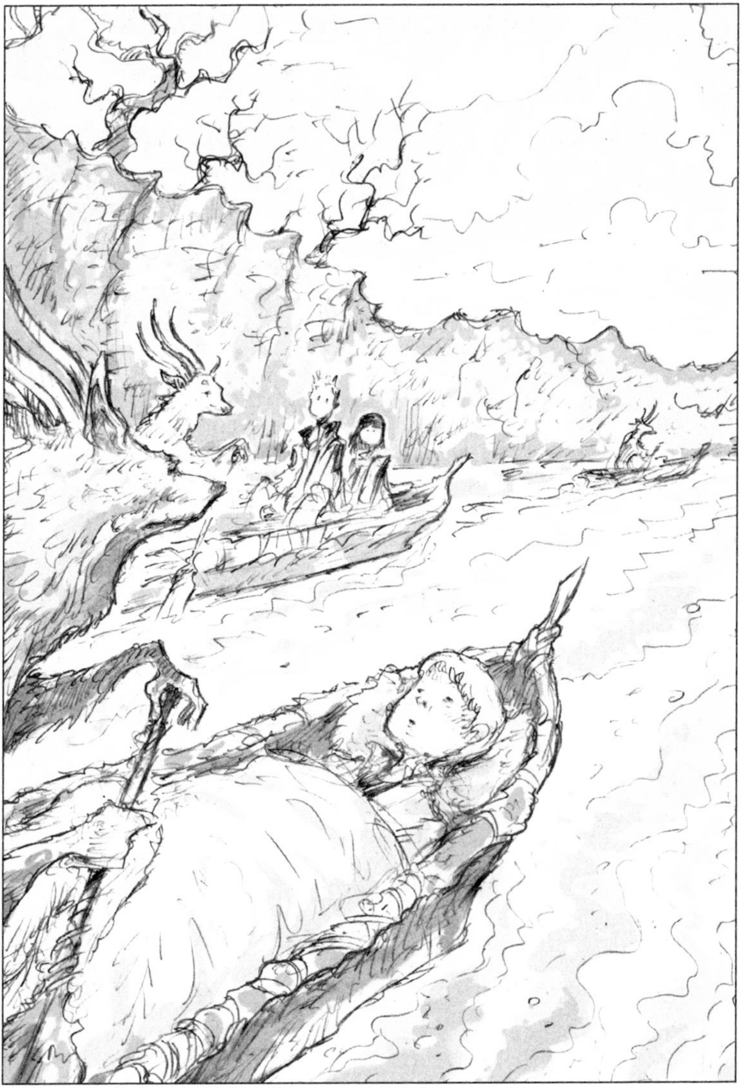

Soon they were off, drifting gently downstream. There was a strong current, so the paddles were used only for steering.

The river grew wider as other streams ran into it. The rocks on the sides of the river gave way to sandy banks.

Chad noticed that no spear plants were growing near the river. He wondered if the soil was too damp for them.

He was still worried about the yellow pollen, for it could travel a long way on the wind. He guessed that the pollen was triggered by noise, like the spears were.

It was a silent place, except for the noise of the wind, which never seemed to stop. It was as if every creature that lived there walked around on tiptoe to avoid upsetting the spear plants.

The horned people's canoes had been designed to be completely silent.

At last the canoes arrived where the river came closest to the base camp. The camp was still about five hundred feet away, and there were still hundreds of spear plants for them to pass.

The horned man who had traveled alone stepped out of his boat. He was carrying something that looked like a drum. He put a blanket over his head, then started to crawl silently toward the spear plants.

Slowly, he moved toward the deadly plants. Chad guessed that the man's blanket was soaked in something that protected him from the pollen. But what about the spears? If the horned man made the slightest noise, it would mean certain death.

The horned man kept crawling, on and on. At last he reached the spear plants. He tucked himself underneath the big leaves. Carefully he reached out from under the blanket and started banging loudly on his drum.

CHAPTER 8

The Shuttle

The other horned man pushed Chad and Sammi down into the boat and threw a stinky blanket over them. Red Arm covered up Jak. They could hear the swish of spears and the thud of them hitting the ground. Then came more drumming, followed by more swishings and thuds, farther away this time.

Sammi felt sick under the smelly blanket. Another minute passed, and the horned man climbed out of the boat.

He tugged on their arms. They stepped out onto the bank, keeping the blanket over their heads.

Sammi realized she could see her way by looking carefully through the cloth.

The air was full of pollen, but the blanket protected them. The drummer came to meet them, still wearing his blanket.

Soon they were walking through the spear plants. The plants had fired off all their spears at the sound of the drumming, so it was safe. Chad was helping Red Arm with Jak's stretcher. When they reached the gate of the camp, the horned men stopped.

It is difficult to say good-bye to people who have helped you so much, especially when you can't speak to them.

Sammi held Red Arm's furry hands and
realized that she didn't need to speak. Sammi
felt like she knew what Red Arm was thinking,
although it was feelings instead of words. And
the feelings said, "Good luck to you. Come
back to us soon."

Chad and Sammi carried Jak to the shuttle. When they reached it, they turned around, but the horned people were gone.

The shuttle door swished open. They squeezed into the tiny airlock, closed the outside door, and waited while the air was changed. This kept them safe from the planet's dangerous pollen.

Finally they were able to throw off the blankets. Chad sat down at the ship's radio. "It might take a while to contact anyone," he said. "It depends how far away *Titan* is."

He flipped the switches. "Chad Mason to *Titan*. Come in, please, *Titan*."

To his surprise, a voice answered almost right away. "*Titan* here. Who is with you? Over."

"I'm with Sammi and Jak Ward. Jak is sick and needs help. Where are you? Over," Chad said.

"We're orbiting behind one of the moons," the voice said.

Chad wasted no time in taking off. As they watched through the shuttle's windows, Chad nudged Sammi and pointed. A star grew brighter. The *Titan*!

As soon as the shuttle was attached to the *Titan*'s dock, people rushed in to get Jak. All three of them were taken straight to the ship's hospital.

The hospital was crowded. Beds full of sleeping people were squeezed in all over the place. In the middle of it all, Mrs. Ward was waiting for them.

Sammi rushed to her, and they both cried.
Her mom looked down at Jak before he was
rushed away. "I thought I had lost my whole
family," Sammi's mother said.

Sammi felt scared. "What do you mean, your whole family? What about Dad?"

Sammi's mother led her to one of the beds. Mr. Ward lay there sleeping, surrounded by flashing machines.

"All of the people from the base are like this. We know it was the pollen from those plants, but the doctors haven't been able to wake them up," said her mom.

"But we know how to," Sammi exclaimed. "The horned people showed us. Quick, get those smelly blankets out of the shuttle!"

A few minutes later a crewman appeared, carrying the rough blankets.

"We were just about to burn these," he said.

Doctors gathered around.

The dirty, smelly blankets looked out of place in the clean hospital. Sammi explained how the horned people used them.

Mr. Ward was the first patient for the treatment. The blanket was laid over him. For a while, nothing happened.

The captain came to see them. He explained why the *Titan* had moved behind the moon.

"You should have remembered the most important rule about exploring space," he said. "Intelligent races of people must be left alone and not disturbed. Meeting a more advanced race can be very dangerous. We've learned that from Earth history. When we first arrived here, we didn't know about the horned people."

"One of the other pilots found them just after you did, so we had to leave quickly," said the captain.

"But what about the flares?" Sammi asked.

The captain looked uncomfortable.

"I wish you hadn't mentioned that. Your mom talked me into using them. The rules don't actually mention flares. Please, Sammi, don't tell anyone we set them off."

Jak woke up first. His arm had almost returned to normal, and his doctor looked very pleased.

"It was a pretty powerful poison," the doctor said. "We soon figured out how to treat it. If we had waited another hour, though, things could have been bad."

Jak and Sammi heard a cheer coming from the bed where Mr. Ward lay. He was waking up!

Their father was weak and groggy, but he was feeling better.

"What happened?" he asked.

Sammi laughed. She didn't know where to start.

The End

About the Author

David Orme, who also writes as David Johnson, taught school for 18 years before becoming a full-time writer. He has written over 200 books about tornadoes, orangutans, soccer, space travel, and other topics. In his free time, David enjoys taking his granddaughter, Sarah, on adventures, climbing nearby mountains, and visiting city graveyards. He lives in Hampshire, England, with his wife, Helen, who is also a writer.

About the Illustrator

Sonny Liew was born in Malaysia, but he now lives in Singapore. He has worked on comics, computer games, and illustrations for many different comic and game publishers. He has been a featured illustrator in the critically-acclaimed *Flight* series. Currently, Liew is working on Disney's "Wonderland."

Glossary

empath (EM-path)—someone who feels for another person; someone who has empathy

empathy (EM-puh-thee)—feeling someone else's feelings as if they were your own

flare (FLAYRE)—a bright light used as a signal

flickering (FLIK-ur-ing)—to move or wave quickly and unsteadily; a candle in the wind burns with a flickering flame.

groggy (GROG-ee)—dizzy, confused

homing signal (HOH-ming SIG-nul)—an electronic sound or light that can lead a person home or to a safe location

loom (LOOM)—a wooden frame used for making cloth

paralyzed (PARE-uh-lyzd)—unable to move

shuttle (SHUT-uhl)—a ship that moves between two places. A shuttle can move people from a planet to a large ship in space.

storehouse (STOR-hows)—a building to keep supplies

Discussion Questions

1. When Sammi first sees a horned person, she screams. She is afraid. What would you do if you saw an alien creature?

2. The aliens in the story were very helpful and caring. On page 58, Chad wishes that humans could be more like them. Do you think humans could learn something from the horned people?

3. Sammi felt as if the horned people could read her mind. Would you like people to be able to read your mind? Why or why not? Would you like to be able to read other people's minds?